# We planted a
# PUMPKIN

A book to share from
**Scallywag Press**

For all the pollinators in the garden who
helped the pumpkin on its way

First published in Great Britain in 2020
by Scallywag Press Ltd, 10 Sutherland Row, London SW1V 4JT

Text and illustration copyright © Rob Ramsden, 2020
The rights of Rob Ramsden to be identified as the author and illustrator
of this work have been asserted by him in accordance with the
Copyright, Designs and Patents Act, 1988

Printed on FSC paper in China by Toppan Leefung

001

British Library Cataloguing in Publication Data available
ISBN 978-1-912650-38-5

# ROB RAMSDEN

# We planted a PUMPKIN

Scallywag Press Ltd
LONDON

This is us.

We planted a seed,
to grow a pumpkin
for Halloween.

Beneath the earth,
a root pushed down.

The sun shone out . . .

two leaves
shot up.

"Go, seed, go!"

"We know you're trying,
each day you're growing,
but oh, too slow . . .

too slow, slow, slow,
to be in time
for Halloween."

Flowers opened,
bugs arrived . . .

bees and lacewings,
butterflies!

The flowers died, except for one.
And underneath . . .

a small green bump!

But it was not a
pumpkin yet.

"Come on, bumpkin!
Go, go, GROW . . .

The bigger,
the fatter,
the BETTER!"

Our pumpkin grew and grew and grew.
It was big and it was fat . . .

But it was GREEN!

"Come on, plumpkin!
Go, go, ORANGE!

You can't be green
for Halloween."

Our pumpkin loved the summer sun.

When it didn't rain,
we were the rain.

Slowly, our pumpkin's
colour changed . . .

The green became less,
the orange more.

"Go, go, PUMPKIN!
Ripen up!"

Our pumpkin listened . . .

It was big and it was fat.
It was orange,
    it was ripe!

But it was HEAVY . . .

"Pull, pull, *PULL!*"

We pushed our pumpkin,

Oh-so-slow . . .

And heaved it onto the tabletop.
We hollowed it out
and carved a face.

Just in time for . . .

Trick or Treating!

Wailing

"Whoooooo..."

and shouting

"BOO!"

On the night of
Halloween.